P9-CKX-595
NO LONGER PROPERTY OF
SEATTLE PUBLIC LIBRARY

Holidays at HOGWARTS

Written by
Elizabeth Dowsett

Contents

LEGO

Introduction

Exploding Wizard Crackers, enchanted decorations, snow falling from the Great Hall ceiling ... Hogwarts School of Witchcraft and Wizardry is magical all year, but in winter it's truly spellbinding. Before Harry Potter was 11 he had no idea he was a wizard, and Christmases with his cruel uncle, aunt, and cousin were miserable. But now he's at Hogwarts, and many mysterious and magical things happen during the holidays ...

HOOT!
HOOT!
Ancient tower soars up into the night sky
Harry's owl, Hedwig, swoops through the snow
The Great Hall hosts the festive feast

Hogwarts winter wonderland

Surrounded by mountains, Hogwarts School of Witchcraft and Wizardry faces harsh weather. Its winters may be very frosty, but they make for dreamy white Christmases. The castle is a welcoming sanctuary for any students who stay here during the holidays.

Stone walls offer magical protection to the castle's inhabitants

Over a thousand Christmases have been celebrated at Hogwarts.

Huge turkey sits on one of the long tables in the Great Hall
CHRISTMAS IS TRULY MAGICAL!
Navy knitted sweater is very cozy
Present wrapped in Gryffindor house colors of scarlet and gold

Harry Potter

After years of Christmases with the cruel Dursley family, Harry gets the chance to spend the festive season at school with his friends. Christmas at Hogwarts is a special time, with huge decorated trees and amazing feasts. Harry even receives proper gifts for the first time in his life!

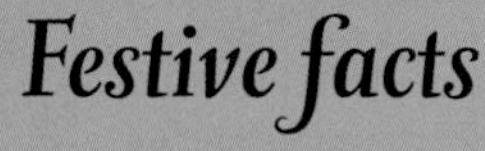

Festive facts

1. Harry spends winter break at Hogwarts for his first four years of school.
2. In his first year, Mrs. Weasley gifts him a knitted sweater with an "H" on it.
3. Harry also receives an Invisibility Cloak. But who is the mystery gift from?

Fantastic food

Hogwarts students and staff enjoy tasty meals all year, but during the holidays the food is particularly delicious and plentiful. The castle isn't full because most students go home for the holidays—and those who stay definitely have their taste buds tantalized!

All the trimmings

The centerpiece of the food festivities is a traditional turkey with mountains of roasted potatoes, gravy, and all the sprouts you can eat.

Pumpkin power

Pumpkins aren't just for Halloween. Pumpkin juice and pumpkin pasties are year-round wizard favorites and holiday essentials.

Crowd pleaser

Mounds of rich, buttery mashed potatoes and a crispy roast chicken leg are nicely rounded off with a tasty Cauldron Cake.

Did you know?

Students sit at four very long tables in the Great Hall—one for each house. Food and drink appear on the tables by magic.

Delicious desserts

Be sure to save room for the final course! There is something for everyone with a sweet tooth, including cupcakes, ice cream, cookies, and elaborate frosted cakes.

Hermione Granger

What's better than Christmas if you're Hermione Granger? Christmas at school! A Hogwarts Christmas is a good time for extra studying or brewing tricky potions. In her first year, Hermione goes home to her Muggle (non-magical) parents, but after that year she often spends the festive season with Harry and Ron.

Jolly Gryffindor Dean Thomas is full of festive cheer

Snow-covered fir tree

Festive facts

1. Hermione declares that Ron and Harry's game of wizard chess is "totally barbaric."
2. She partly transforms herself into a cat by accident during the holidays of their second year.
3. She goes to the Yule Ball event with Quidditch star Viktor Krum in her fourth year.

MY WORK IS LOOKING TREE-MENDOUS!
Woolly scarf in Gryffindor-colored stripes
Ornament can be levitated up the tree with the *Wingardium Leviosa* charm

O Christmas tree!

During the holidays, Hogwarts brings the outside inside with fir trees from the castle grounds. Traditionally, the Great Hall has twelve trees, with a particularly huge one in the largest window. Wizards decorate their trees like Muggles do, but with a magical twist.

Snowed up

This lush fir tree, decorated with shiny glass ornaments and magical snow, brings festive cheer to Hogwarts.

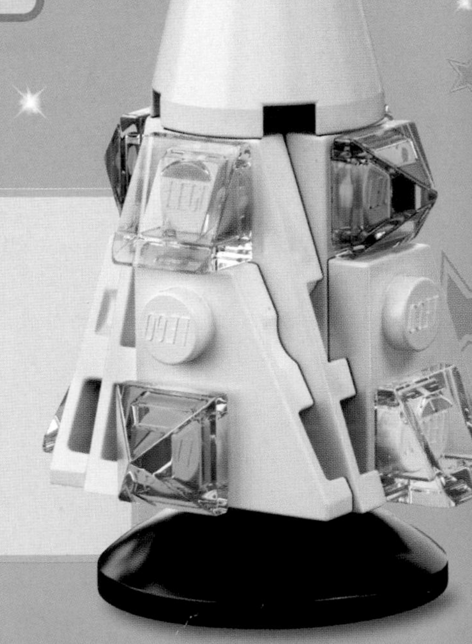

Yule trees

Blue-and-white frosted trees decorate the ice-themed Yule Ball that takes place during Harry's fourth year.

Did you know?

The Christmas tree in the kitchen at 12 Grimmauld Place has magical snow constantly falling on it.

Star quality

Decorated with enchanted ornaments, this glossy tree gets the gold star for elegant simplicity.

Keeper of keys and trees

Felling enormous trees and dragging them into the castle is not a problem for Hagrid. He is a strong half-giant and Hogwarts' groundskeeper.

Ron Weasley

The sixth of seven children, Ron Weasley is used to noisy family holidays. But in his first year, his parents visit his brother Charlie in Romania, so Ron has a calmer Christmas at Hogwarts with Harry. Free from lessons, they relax by playing wizard chess.

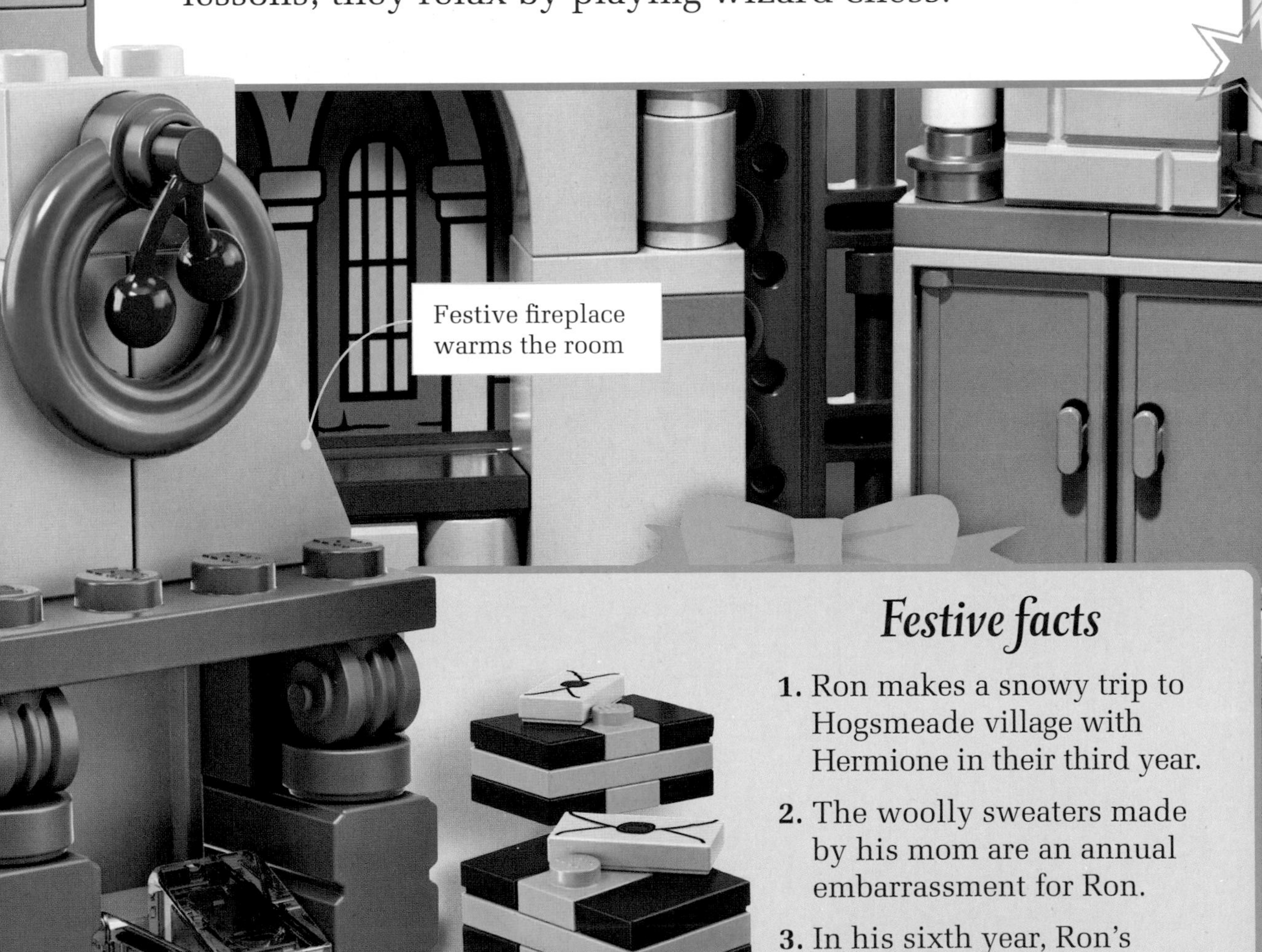

Festive fireplace warms the room

Festive facts

1. Ron makes a snowy trip to Hogsmeade village with Hermione in their third year.
2. The woolly sweaters made by his mom are an annual embarrassment for Ron.
3. In his sixth year, Ron's girlfriend, Lavender, gives "Won Won" a heart-shaped necklace.

HARRY CHRISTMAS, EVERYONE!
Fir tree felled and brought into the castle by Hagrid
"R" for "Ron" sweater knitted with love
Goblet of spiced pumpkin juice

Festive fun and games

In their first year, Harry and Ron have a lot of time on their hands when lessons stop and Hermione goes home for the holidays. Ron teaches Harry to play wizard chess. It takes a lot of practice and skill to play it well, but you never know when it will come in handy.

Long Gryffindor table is the perfect setting for a board game

Harry and Ron get ready to hone their chess skills in the quiet Great Hall.

Did you know?
Wizard chess is a bit like Muggle chess, but the pieces move themselves and actually smash each other up.
Ron tells his pieces where to go and then they move
GAME ON, HARRY!
NOT FOR ME, I'M HEADING HOME. SEE YOU NEXT YEAR!
Hermione's trunk is packed and ready
Enchanted pieces can even offer players advice

The season of giving

In his first year, Harry is amazed to discover that he has been given gifts—no one has ever given him a Christmas present before. Not only does Harry receive some great things to unwrap, but he has special people in his life now who want to give him presents.

Priceless present

For Harry's first Christmas at Hogwarts, he is given a very rare and valuable gift—an Invisibility Cloak. It belonged to his father.

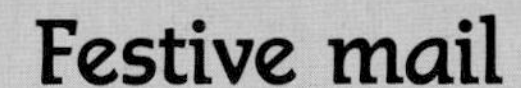

Festive mail

Cards are strung up in Ron and Harry's dormitory and pinned on the Gryffindor common room's noticeboard. They bring season's greetings from friends and family.

Chocolate treats

There's no tastier gift than a Chocolate Frog! Each one comes with a card of a famous witch or wizard. Just be sure to eat your frog before it jumps away!

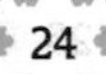

Magical map

Just before the winter holidays in Harry's third year, Fred and George Weasley pass the Marauder's Map on to him. It reveals where everybody is in the castle—useful for creeping around without getting caught.

Did you know?

To reveal the map's secrets, you must tap it with your wand and say, "I solemnly swear that I am up to no good."

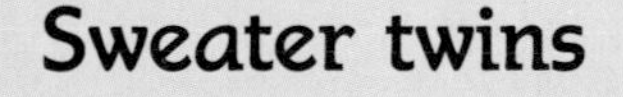

Sweater twins

The Weasleys can't afford extravagant gifts, but Mrs. Weasley's personalized sweaters are knitted with wool and lots of love.

Nighttime adventure

On Christmas night, Harry uses his new gift. The Invisibility Cloak is just what he needs to sneak into the library's Restricted Section after dark. But grumpy school caretaker Filch is around, too, and it would make his Christmas to punish a student for being out of bed.

Typical frowning expression

Lantern lights Filch's way, but it can't reveal invisible Harry

Old books are
full of dark,
magical secrets
Could this
book reveal the
information
Harry wants?
I NEED EVERY
TRICK IN THE
BOOK.
The Restricted Section
of the library is out of
bounds to students
without permission.

Bright-eyed owl is ready for its next delivery
Perches for Hogwarts' own owls, students' owls, and visiting owls
THIS DELIVERY IS IMPORTANT. DON'T JUST WING IT!
Letters, newspapers, and even packages are all carried by owl
The cold and noisy Owlery is located at the top of the West Tower.

Hogwarts delivery hub

The wizarding world relies on owls to deliver mail, so winter is a flurry of feathery activity. The castle's Owlery is a sanctuary for busy birds. But be warned: if you've been naughty this year, an owl may bring you a Howler—a screeching, angry message!

Tired owls rest after long journeys to and from the castle

Hedwig

Proud and loyal Hedwig is Harry's animal companion and friend. She carries his mail and lives in the Owlery. As a snowy owl, Hedwig is comfortable with Hogwarts' cold winters. Harry watches her gliding through the falling snowflakes, high up in the sky.

Feathered wings can flap almost silently

Blue gloves keep Harry's hands toasty warm

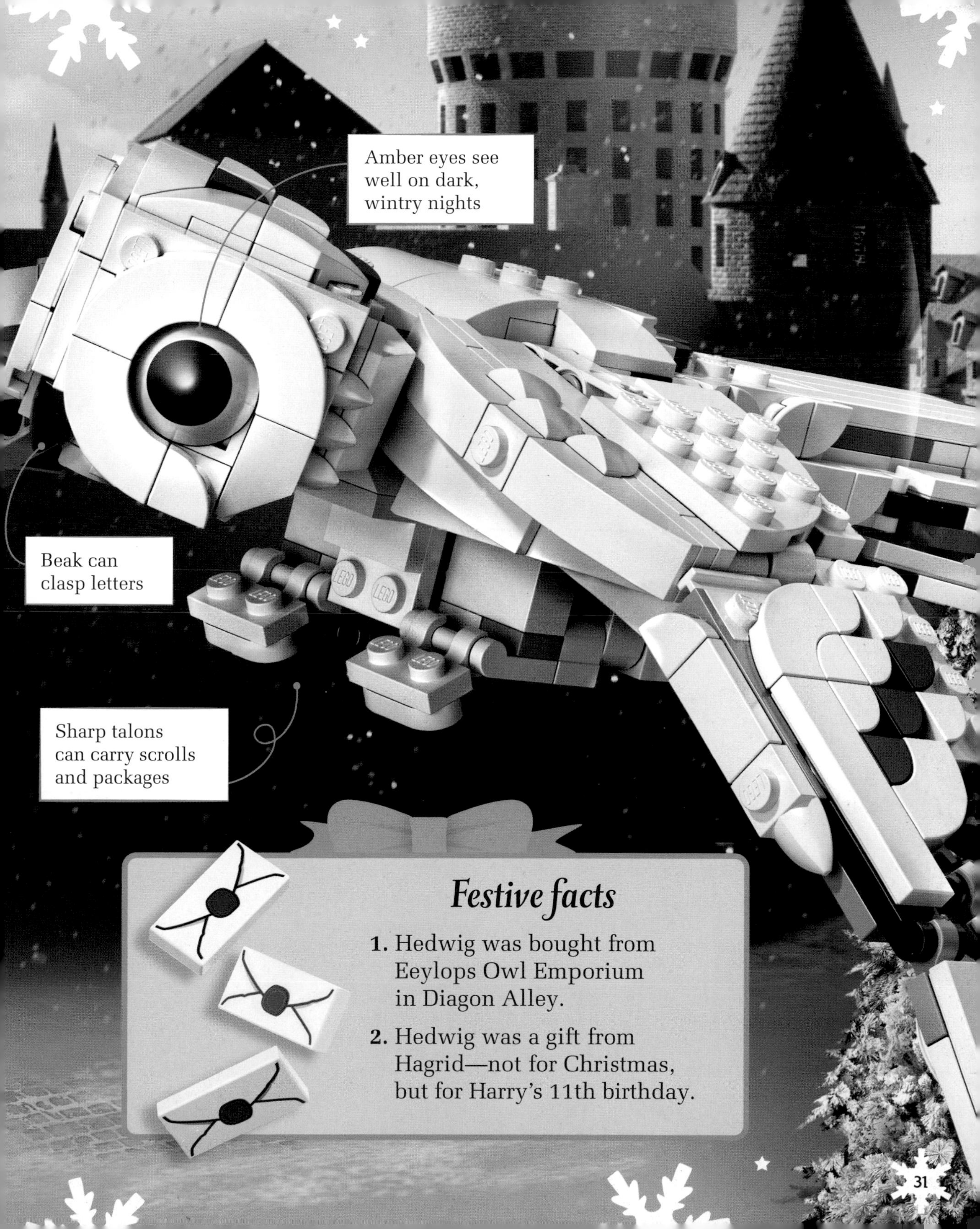

Festive facts

1. Hedwig was bought from Eeylops Owl Emporium in Diagon Alley.
2. Hedwig was a gift from Hagrid—not for Christmas, but for Harry's 11th birthday.

Holiday wishes

Harry stumbles upon a magical mirror on Christmas night as he tries to avoid Filch, the caretaker. The Mirror of Erised reflects not reality, but a person's deepest desires. The happiest wizard in the world would look in the mirror and see themselves, just as they are.

Simple pleasures

Dumbledore claims his reflection shows him holding a nice warm pair of woolly socks. After all, you can never have enough socks!

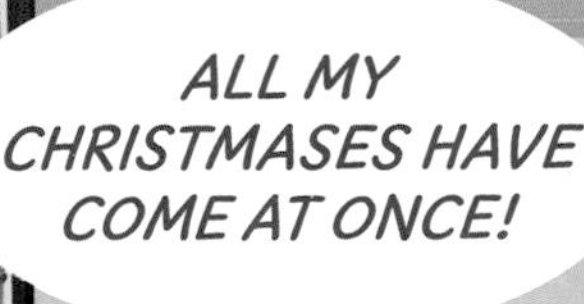

Winning streak

In the mirror, Ron outshines his five older brothers. He has become both Quidditch Captain and head boy, and is holding the House Cup.

Did you know?

The name of the mirror is carved in the top of the frame. Erised is "desire" backward—as it would appear in a mirror.

Family portrait

Harry can't remember his parents because they died when he was a baby. He sees himself standing with them as they smile lovingly at him.

Transformation time

Rather than hot chocolate, Ron and Harry drink revolting Polyjuice Potion during their second Christmas at Hogwarts. It turns them briefly into Crabbe and Goyle—friends of vile bully Draco Malfoy—as part of a plan to find out Malfoy's secrets.

Gloomy ghost Moaning Myrtle watches what the students are up to

Bubbling Polyjuice Potion is very tricky to make

After a month of brewing, Hermione's potion is finally ready.

Deserted girls' bathroom is a good place to brew secret potions
THAT LOOKS ... DELICIOUS?! AFTER YOU, HARRY!
Cupcakes contain sleeping draft for the real Crabbe and Goyle

The picturesque village is especially pretty under its blanket of snow.

Festive trips

Hogwarts students are allowed to visit the nearby village of Hogsmeade, if their parents or guardians give permission. In December, they can buy presents in Honeydukes sweet shop, and weary shoppers can have a refreshing drink in The Three Broomsticks inn. Harry has no permission so he visits in secret!

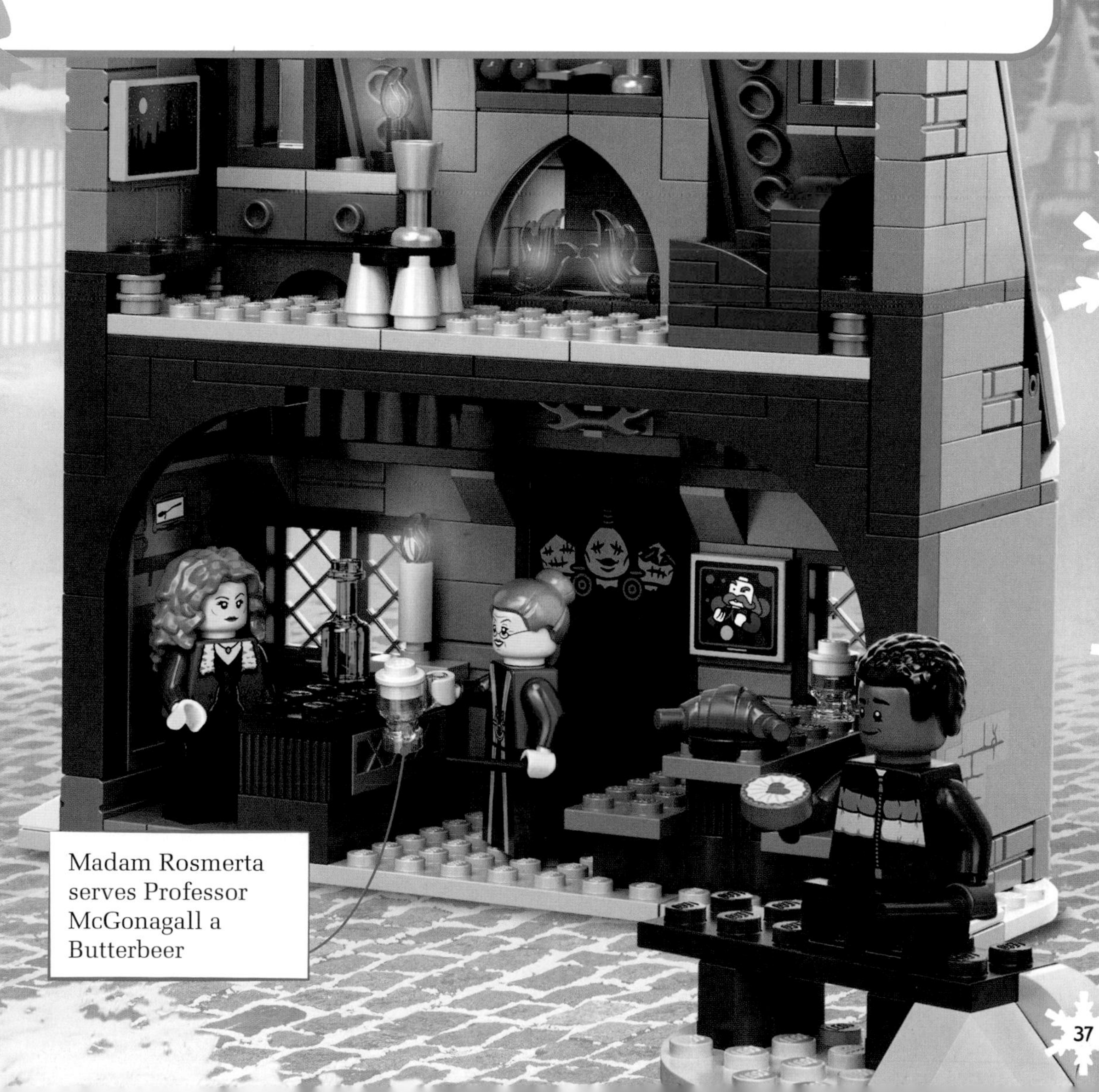

Madam Rosmerta serves Professor McGonagall a Butterbeer

Snowball attack

In Harry's third year, the winter visit to Hogsmeade village doesn't go as planned when Ron and Hermione are cornered by spiteful Draco Malfoy near the Shrieking Shack. Fortunately Harry is under his Invisibility Cloak and he scares Malfoy away with a shower of spooky snowballs.

Smug expression is about to be wiped off Malfoy's face

Snowball thrown by an invisible hand

The unsuspecting Malfoy is surprised by a mystery foe.

Shrieking Shack is said to be the most haunted building in Britain
AVALANCHE INCOMING!
Cloak helps Harry sneak around Hogsmeade unseen

Holiday guests

In Harry's fourth year, Hogwarts hosts the Triwizard Tournament—a legendary competition between the three main wizarding schools of Europe. Hogwarts welcomes visitors from Beauxbatons Academy of Magic and Durmstrang Institute. May the best school win! The guests stay all year, including the festive season.

Triwizard Cup will be awarded to the winner

Fleur Delacour competes for Beauxbatons

The guests live in the school grounds and join feasts in the Great Hall.

Did you know?

1. Normally only one champion represents each school.
2. Harry's name was secretly submitted on his behalf into the tournament. He is magically bound to compete.
3. Three dangerous tasks test the champions' magical skill, intelligence, and bravery.

Cedric Diggory from Hufflepuff is the original Hogwarts champion

Viktor Krum represents Durmstrang

WHAT'S UP, HARRY?

Harry holds a poster for the Yule Ball event. This part of the Triwizard Tournament is all about having fun and making friends with students from other wizarding schools.
I'M HAVING A BALL!
YULE BALL
The Weird Sisters

Welcome to the ball!

For the Yule Ball on Christmas Eve, the Great Hall is transformed into a wintery wonderland with a dance floor and elegant ice sculptures. The usual long trestle tables are replaced with sociable round tables for the feast. Let the celebrations begin!

Beauxbatons' headmistress, Madame Maxime, dances with Dumbledore

A glass of delicious pumpkin juice

Partygoers waltz in pairs on the dance floor.

DO YOU KNOW THE HIPPOGRIFF HOP?
Icicles hang down from the refreshments table

Dressed to impress

The fancy Yule Ball is an occasion for everyone to dress up in their finest clothes and dance the night away in a swirl of robes, shimmer, and sparkle. Apart from poor Ron, who thinks his old-fashioned dress robes make him look (and smell) like his great-aunt Tessie!

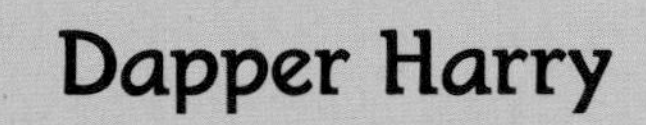

Dapper Harry

Harry's brand-new dress robes make him look very handsome. They include a black dinner jacket with tails, a white dress shirt, and a white bow tie.

Wronged Ron

Ron is very embarrassed by his frilly, second-hand dress robes. His bad mood is also caused by Hermione going to the ball with Viktor Krum.

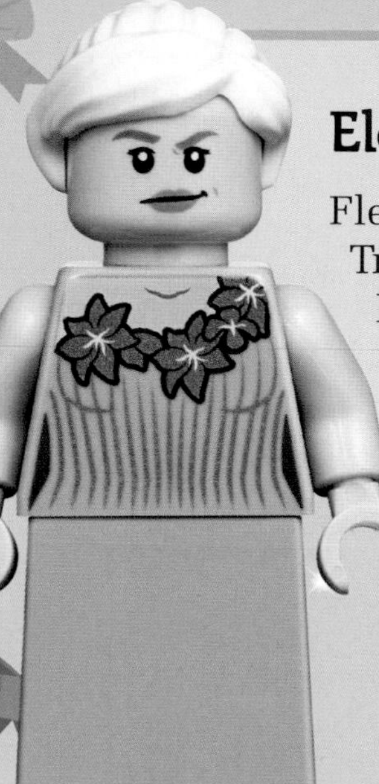

Elegant Fleur

Fleur forgets the difficult and dangerous Triwizard Tournament for one night. Her dancing skills and her delicate gray dress are both enchanting.

Stunning Hermione

Hermione turns heads when she makes her entrance in her dress robes. Her hair is elegantly styled and her layered pink gown makes her the belle of the ball.

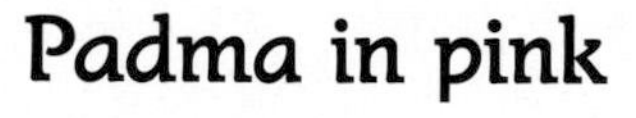

Padma in pink

Padma Patil's embroidered robes are the same as those of her twin, Parvati, but with reversed colors. Padma's partner is Ron, but he is too grumpy to be any fun.

Did you know?

It's a Yule Ball tradition that the Triwizard competitors and their partners open the ball by dancing first.

Filius Flitwick

Professor Filius Flitwick teaches Charms and is Head of Ravenclaw house. He uses his impressive skill to decorate the Hogwarts Christmas trees by levitating ornaments into place. Highly musical, Flitwick also conducts the school orchestra and the choir at important events.

Sheet music for the waltz that opens the ball

Piano is played at the Yule Ball as part of the orchestra

Microphone for the lead singer of the Weird Sisters band

Festive facts
1. Flitwick's orchestra opens the Yule Ball.
2. At the ball, Flitwick introduces famous wizard rock band the Weird Sisters.
3. The spirited professor crowd-surfs during the Weird Sisters' performance.
Ornaments are held on the tree with Flitwick's charms
CHARMING, QUITE CHARMING.
Enchanted megaphone magically boosts Flitwick's voice

Deck the halls

Hogwarts is a grand and beautiful building, but its stone walls can be a little bare. For the holidays, the castle becomes more festive with twinkling ornaments and lush boughs of holly. The jolly decorations make Hogwarts look just as magical as it is.

All in the detail

Enchanted, ever-burning candles, shiny ornaments, and glittering golden stars add sparkle to every tree and gloomy corner.

Cozy stockings

Stockings are hung up in anticipation of gifts like Cauldron Cakes, Bertie Bott's Every Flavor Beans, or even Fred and George Weasley's Skiving Snackbox joke kits.

Green touch

Boughs of evergreen foliage from the castle grounds cheer up the short, dark days—especially prickly holly leaves with their bright red berries.

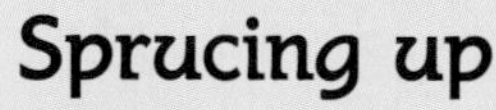

Sprucing up

Festive wreaths and garlands brighten up stone pillars and arches. They also add a pop of color to the dark wood paneling in Hogwarts' corridors and the entrance hall.

Did you know?

The ceiling of the Great Hall is enchanted to match the sky and weather outside, including falling snow.

Ice sculpture

Frosty tables dripping with icicles adorn the Yule Ball. This one holds a magnificent ice sculpture centerpiece—an onion-domed fairy-tale castle.

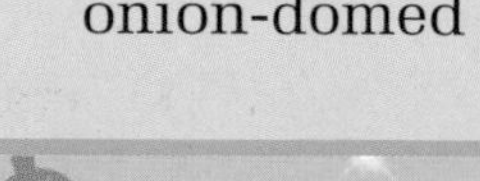

Eccentric tasseled hat in a pale gold color
LET'S TALK TURKEY!
Long dress robes have detailed embroidery

Albus Dumbledore

Professor Albus Percival Wulfric Brian Dumbledore is the headmaster of Hogwarts. As a permanent resident of the castle, Dumbledore usually spends the winter holidays here—although he does spend it away from Hogwarts on a mysterious trip in Harry's sixth year.

Crispy roasted potatoes

Dumbledore sits at the teachers' high table

Festive facts

1. Dumbledore is the anonymous gifter who gives Harry the Invisibility Cloak.
2. At the Yule Ball, he dances with Professor McGonagall.
3. Dumbledore finds Harry looking into the Mirror of Erised on Christmas night in Harry's first year.

Secret headquarters

In Harry's fifth year, there is a problem in the weeks leading up to winter break. Where can a group of students—called Dumbledore's Army—practice forbidden Defense Against the Dark Arts spells in safety? Luckily, Hogwarts has the answer: the Room of Requirement. The room only appears when someone has real need of it.

Wheeled dummy for dueling practice

Hermione's Patronus takes the form of an otter

Luna Lovegood's hare Patronus leaps through the air
HARE'S MY PATRONUS!
Candle-covered tree gives a festive air
The room provides students with everything they need to practice magic.

Mistletoe could contain mischievous Nargle creatures
Tarnished mirror with notices and pictures
ALBUS DUMBLEDORE ?
IS THIS THE END FOR
HARRY, YOU'RE MY CHOSEN ONE.
Blue-and-silver Ravenclaw uniform

Under the mistletoe

After Dumbledore's Army's final training session of term, Cho Chang hangs back to see Harry. It is their last chance for time together before the winter break. The Room of Requirement is the perfect space for learning defensive magic—and also for alone time.

Disheveled tie from practicing Stunning spells

Harry and Cho have been admiring each other all term.

Molly Weasley

Ron's mom, Molly, is warm and kind as she fusses over her large brood. She and Arthur Weasley have seven children, and Harry is like an extra member of the family. Guests make more work for Mrs. Weasley, but they also make her home even more festive.

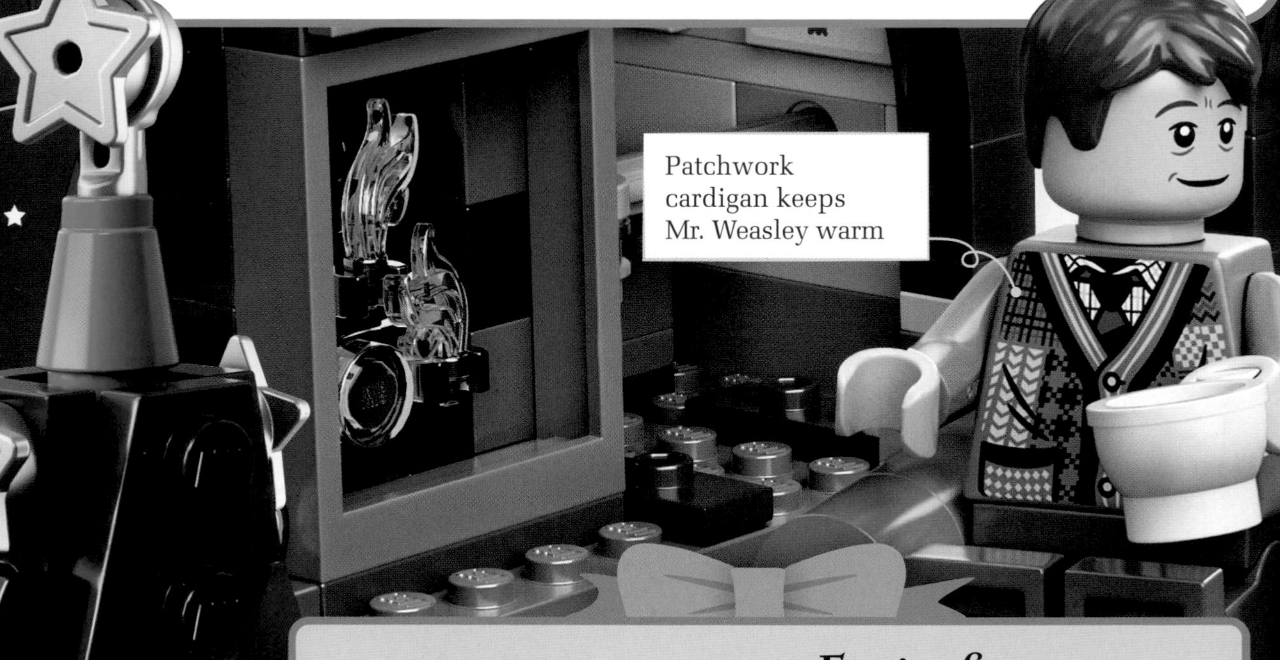

Festive facts

1. Mrs. Weasley knits Ron an unfashionable vest for Christmas in his fifth year.
2. She gifts Fred and George homemade scarves the same year.
3. The Weasleys' cake has an enchanted snowman ice skating on top in Ron's sixth year.

Roof tiles are crooked, just like the entire frame of the house
CHRISTMAS WITH THE WEASLEYS IS A WHEEZE!
Red hair like all the Weasley family
Cluttered table in chaotic but cozy home

Ron's sister, Ginny, helps decorate the dull old house
Stack of presents for the Weasleys and members of the Order

12 Grimmauld Place

In their fifth year, Harry, Ron, and Hermione find festive cheer in the secret headquarters of the Order of the Phoenix—a group sworn to oppose Voldemort and his Dark forces. The headquarters at 12 Grimmauld Place are a safe place to celebrate Christmas among friends.

Table weighed down by even more gifts

Mrs. Weasley's tea comforts everyone

ARE ANY OF THOSE PRESENTS KNITTED?

The house belongs to Harry's godfather, Sirius Black.

Slug Club party time

Potions master Professor Slughorn invites the most impressive students to be in his exclusive "Slug Club." He collects interesting, clever, and famous people like ingredients for his rare potions. In Harry's sixth year, Slughorn hosts a party for his club.

Dapper three-piece suit, chain, and bow tie

Paper lanterns decorate the lavish party

WATCH OUT FOR NARGLES IN THE MISTLETOE.
Luna's ruffled dress is layered like an evergreen tree
Chocolate fountain tops extravagant food display
Dragon tartare is best avoided—it gives the eater bad breath!
Slughorn's party is the highlight of his club's social calendar.

Neville Longbottom

Shy Neville Longbottom finds his confidence on the dance floor and is the first boy to volunteer in the dance classes for the Yule Ball. In his sixth year, before going home to spend Christmas with his grandmother as usual, Neville works as a waiter at the Slug Club party.

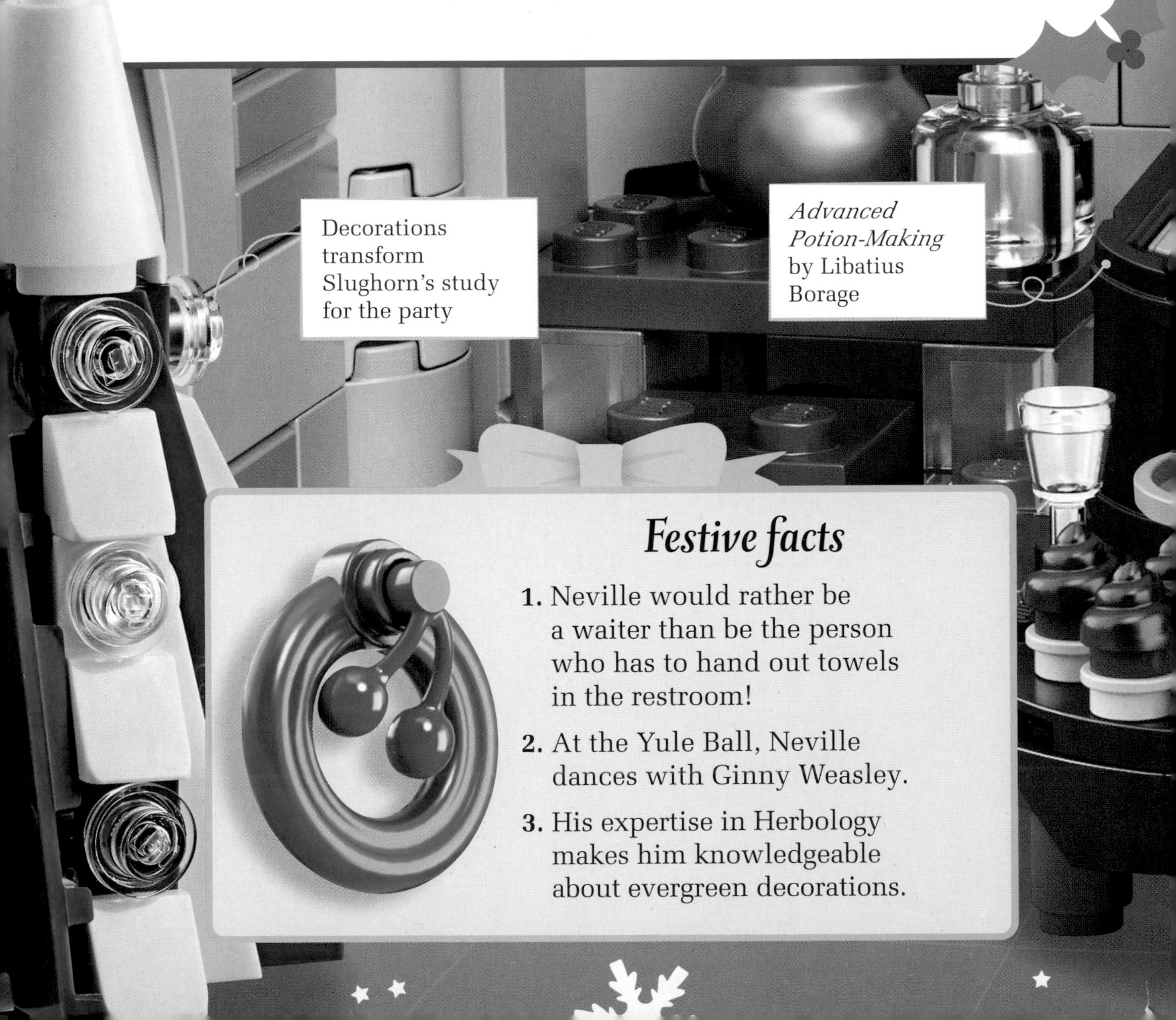

Decorations transform Slughorn's study for the party

Advanced Potion-Making by Libatius Borage

Festive facts

1. Neville would rather be a waiter than be the person who has to hand out towels in the restroom!
2. At the Yule Ball, Neville dances with Ginny Weasley.
3. His expertise in Herbology makes him knowledgeable about evergreen decorations.

PUMPKIN JUICE?
Anxious expression
Formal waiter's uniform, with white gloves and gold buttons

Did you know?

Lavender Brown is besotted with her boyfriend, Ron. She draws a heart and "R+L" on a steamed-up train window.

Lavender searches through the train for Ron

Coal tender holds luggage rather than coal because the train runs on magic

The scarlet train steams through the British countryside, unseen by Muggles.

Ho ho home for the holidays

The Hogwarts Express is best known for its 11am departure from platform 9¾ at King's Cross on the first of September, but the train also delivers students back to London for the winter break. Its gleaming red design is known to all witches and wizards.

Gold-topped chimney

Large wheels roll over snowy track

Christmas at The Burrow

The Weasleys' loveable crooked wizard house is near Ottery St. Catchpole in Devon. Over the holidays it is full of Weasleys and their many friends. Hermione, Harry, and Order of the Phoenix members Lupin and Tonks are all welcomed in Harry's sixth year.

Mealtimes at The Burrow are crowded and lively.

Magical clock shows the status or location of each family member
Floo powder for traveling through the fireplace Floo Network

Uninvited visitors

In Harry's sixth year, some visitors who arrive at The Burrow are not so welcome. After dinner, two Death Eaters (followers of Voldemort) appear and torch the surrounding fields. They make cruel taunts and then vanish, leaving The Burrow ablaze.

Ring of fire around the house is ignited by Bellatrix

Harry is the first to dash out of the building to fight

ANYONE WANT TO ROAST SOME CHESTNUTS?
Bellatrix Lestrange arrives in thick plumes of black smoke
Fiery destruction engulfs The Burrow on Christmas Day.
Bloodthirsty werewolf Fenrir Greyback prowls near the house

CANCEL CHRISTMAS, I SAY!
Face glares with suspicion
Keys for opening doors without magic
LEGO
LEGO

Argus Filch

Hogwarts caretaker and grumpy grinch Argus Filch patrols the castle with his cat, Mrs. Norris. He is usually scowling and complaining about the students. When he catches a child breaking even the slightest rule, you would think all his Christmases had come at once!

Festive facts

1. Prowling Filch almost catches Harry in the library on Christmas night.
2. He dances with Mrs. Norris at the Yule Ball.
3. Eagle-eyed Filch captures Draco Malfoy lurking outside Slughorn's party.

Another calendar year at Hogwarts is over! It's time for the holidays—and goodwill to all wizards, witches, and Muggles.
CHRISTMAS? I READ ABOUT THAT IN LEGO® HARRY POTTER™: HOLIDAYS AT HOGWARTS.
HERMIONE, THIS IS NO TIME FOR HOMEWORK!

MERRY CHRISTMAS, EVERYONE!
H

Senior Editor Ruth Amos
Designer Rosamund Bird
Project Art Editor Jenny Edwards
Production Editor Siu Yin Chan
Production Controller Louise Daly
Managing Editor Paula Regan
Managing Art Editor Jo Connor
Publishing Director Mark Searle

DK would like to thank Sam Bartlett for jacket design, Julia March for proofreading, and Megan Douglass for Americanization.

First American Edition, 2021
Published in the United States by DK Publishing
1450 Broadway, Suite 801, New York, NY 10018

21 22 23 24 25 10 9 8 7 6 5 4 3 2 1
001-321875-Sep/2021

Manufactured by Dorling Kindersley, One Embassy Gardens, 8 Viaduct Gardens, London SW11 7BW, under license from the LEGO Group.

A catalog record for this book is available from the Library of Congress.
ISBN 978-0-7440-2863-8
978-0-7440-4012-8 (library edition)

DK books are available at special discounts when purchased in bulk for sales promotions, premiums, fund-raising, or educational use.
For details, contact: DK Publishing Special Markets,
1450 Broadway, Suite 801, New York, NY 10018
SpecialSales@dk.com

Printed and bound in China

For the curious

www.dk.com
www.LEGO.com

This book was made with Forest Stewardship Council ™ certified paper—one small step in DK's commitment to a sustainable future. For more information go to www.dk.com/our-green-pledge